Copyright © 1995 by Nord-Süd Verlag AG, Gossau Zürich, Switzerland
First published in Switzerland under the title *Simons Weihnacht*
English translation copyright © 1995 by North-South Books Inc.

First published in the United States, Great Britain, Canada,
Australia, and New Zealand in 1995 by North-South Books,
an imprint of Nord-Süd Verlag AG, Gossau Zürich, Switzerland.

Distributed in the United States by North-South Books Inc., New York.

Library of Congress Cataloging-in-Publication Data
Lussert, Anneliese.
[Simons Weihnacht. English]
The Christmas Visitor / by Anneliese Lussert;
illustrated by Loek Koopmans; translated by Rosemary Lanning.
Summary: Simon expects a visit from a king and a royal reward
for his hospitality, but when a beggar turns up at his door instead,
he learns the satisfaction of giving.
[1. Jesus Christ—Nativity—Fiction.   2. Generosity—Fiction]
I. Koopmans, Loek, ill.   II. Lanning, Rosemary.   III. Title.
PZ7.L979178Ch 1995
[E]—dc20 95-1642

A CIP catalogue record for this book
is available from The British Library.

ISBN 1-55858-449-8 (trade binding)
1 3 5 7 9 TB 10 8 6 4 2
ISBN 1-55858-450-1 (library binding)
1 3 5 7 9 LB 10 8 6 4 2
Printed in Belgium

The Christmas Visitor

By Anneliese Lussert · Illustrated by Loek Koopmans

TRANSLATED BY ROSEMARY LANNING

North-South Books

NEW YORK · LONDON

THE VILLAGE STREET WAS EMPTY and still. Snow drifted silently from the darkening midwinter sky, and a few birds huddled together in the bare trees.

There was no one about. Who would venture outside in this cold—especially when there was news to share by the fireside, news that a king would visit that night!

Suddenly a door opened. Someone came out and stared up and down the street. It was Simon, the richest man in the village, looking for the royal procession, wanting to make sure it would stop at *his* house. But nothing came.

Simon went back indoors and called to his wife, Sarah. "I'm expecting a visitor," he told her. "Put a candle in every window to help him find us. Then go and cook a meal fit for a king."

Simon's wife was weak and ill. Slowly and painfully she went from room to room, placing a lighted candle on every windowsill.

As Sarah came to the last window, she heard a loud knocking. She hobbled to the door and opened it.

On the doorstep stood a tall, thin man, dressed in rags.

"I seek shelter for myself and my newborn son," he said. "Will you let us in?"

Simon looked at the stranger's ragged clothes and said, "I'll have no beggars in my house!"

"You would be well rewarded for your kindness," said the man.

"You're rich then, are you?" said Simon scornfully.

"I can give you the greatest gifts of all, but I have no money," the stranger replied.

"A poor beggar, just as I thought," said Simon. "I can't have the likes of you loitering around. I'm expecting an important and wealthy guest. Be off with you!"

"Oh, Simon," said Sarah. "We cannot send this poor man out into the cold without at least giving him something to warm his stomach." With that, Sarah led the stranger inside and brought him food and drink. Then she offered him her shawl. "Take it," she said, gazing at him. "It is all I have to give."

"Let me have this, also," said the stranger, gently taking her stick away. "You no longer need it." Then he turned and went out of the house.

Simon stared at his wife. "What has happened to you?" he said. "You're standing so straight."

"I am well again," she exclaimed. "The pain has gone. The stranger has healed me."

"Impossible!" said Simon. "He was only a beggar."

Suddenly Simon remembered the stranger's words: *I can give you the greatest gifts of all.* Could he have been the king in disguise? "What have I done?" he cried. "I must bring him back!"

He put on his cloak and boots and ran after the stranger.

Simon heard someone calling his name from far away. He followed a trail of footprints in the snow, but didn't find the stranger. Instead he saw an old woman, crying. On any other night, Simon would have turned and walked straight past her, but now, to his surprise, he stopped and asked, "What is the matter?"

"I am so cold," she moaned. Simon remembered the stranger's great gift to Sarah and his own rudeness, and suddenly ashamed, he wrapped his cloak around the old woman, then hurried on.

Next he found a small boy, and he was crying too. The boy had no shoes and his feet were red with cold. Once again, Simon was surprised by his own reaction.

He immediately pulled off his own boots and warm socks and gave them to the boy. Barefoot now, Simon walked off without waiting to be thanked.

Again someone called his name. This time it sounded closer, but still he saw no one, so he kept following the tracks in the snow.

When he had walked a little farther, he found an old man sitting under a tree. The man had no coat, and was shivering. Without hesitating, Simon took off his own jacket and gave it to him.

Now Simon was so cold that he was in pain, but the pain did not seem to matter. Inside him was a warmth he had never known before.

Again someone called his name, and this time the voice seemed to come from just ahead of him.

There stood the stranger Simon had turned away. Now he was dressed in rich blue robes, no longer a beggar, but a king, with a radiance that shone around him.

The king said, "Simon, you have passed the test I set for you. Follow my footprints a little farther and you will find my son, waiting for you."

Simon did as he was told.

He followed the footprints and came to a stable.

Inside was a newborn child, cradled by straw, lying in a manger.
The stable glowed with warm light. Awed and afraid, Simon knelt
and began to pray.

Then the child looked up and welcomed him with a smile, a smile that filled Simon's heart with peace and love and joy, which are indeed the greatest gifts of all.